My Best Friends

For: Susan and Ralph
From: A.T.B.

First published in Great Britain in 2003
by Zero To Ten, part of Evans Publishing Group
2A Portman Mansions
Chiltern Street
London W1U 6NR
Copyright © 2003 Zero To Ten Ltd
Text copyright © 2003 Anna Nilsen
Illustrations copyright © 2003 Emma Dodd

 **Children's Publishing**

This edition published in the
United States of America in 2003 by
Gingham Dog Press
an imprint of McGraw-Hill Children's Publishing,
a Division of The McGraw-Hill Companies
8787 Orion Place
Columbus, Ohio 43240-4027

www.MHkids.com

ISBN 0-7696-3159-2

Library of Congress Cataloging-in-Publication Data is on file with the publisher.

Printed in China.

1 2 3 4 5 6 7 8 9 10 EVN 09 08 07 06 05 04 03

My Best Friends

By Anna Nilsen
Illustrated by Emma Dodd

GINGHAM DOG
PRESS

Columbus, Ohio

Best friends smile and say hello

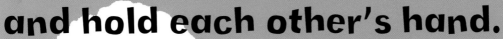
and hold each other's hand.

Best friends laugh and dance at parties

Best friends give each other presents

and share their favorite toys.

Best friends put on grown-ups'
shoes when they play
dress-up.

and swoosh and splash in wading pools.

Best friends take each other home for a snack and always share their treats and candy.

Best friends sometimes get mad and fight

but soon make up
with a hug.

**Best friends get tired
and angry**

Best friends tell each other secrets.

Some best friends stay friends forever.